To all the Baby Boos...Sleep Sweet
~xoxo

Sleep Sweet xoxo
Copyright ©2012 by Patsy Clairmont

Published in Franklin, Tennessee by Patsy Clairmont.

Text copyright ©2012 by Patsy Clairmont.
Illustration copyright ©2012 by Shelley Johannes.

Book design by Shelley Johannes.
Illustrations were rendered in watercolor and ink.

First Edition, 2012.

ISBN 978-0-9834002-6-4

Printed in the United States of America.

www.PatsyClairmont.com

PATSY CLAIRMONT

ILLUSTRATED BY SHELLEY JOHANNES

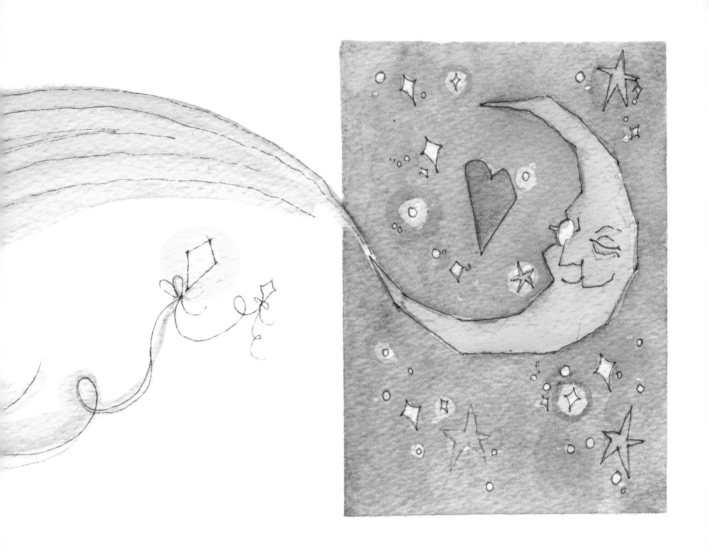

Slice of moon lean into the night,
pour me your tea full of dreams and starlight.
Whisper secrets in wind song and dew,
tell me your mysteries...give me a clue.

*H*ow do you smile
when you're up so high?

*A*re the stars your good friends twinkling nearby?
Do you call them by name like Paige, Ben, and Boo?
Do you ever play games like skip-to-my-loo?

Moon thank-you for
sprinkling light on my bed,
while warming the pillow
under my head.

Sometimes I catch
a beam in my hand

*A*nd pretend
I'm a captain
leading a band.

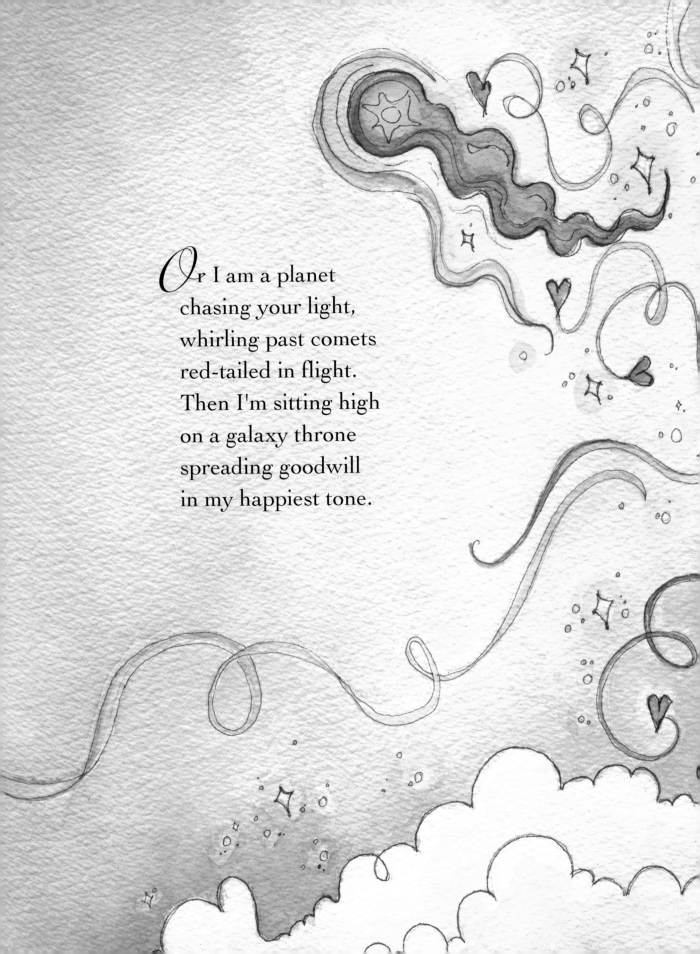

*O*r I am a planet
chasing your light,
whirling past comets
red-tailed in flight.
Then I'm sitting high
on a galaxy throne
spreading goodwill
in my happiest tone.

*A*fter you slip
behind a puffy-faced cloud,
I giggle hard,
trying not to be loud.

"Mr. Moon" I say,
    in my whispery way,
        "Come out, Come out, can we still play?"

*Y*es, yes, I know it's late
and time to sleep,
under the heavens
and blankets so deep.
So I'll close my eyes
and be perfectly still
while you sip warm tea
and drink your fill.

*B*ut tomorrow promise
with all your might
you'll come again
with another goodnight.
Cause I like the way
you dance round the bed
and press
rainbow kisses
atop my head.

*N*ight-night Mr. Moon
who paints the dark sky
and sparkles the earth
as it circles by.

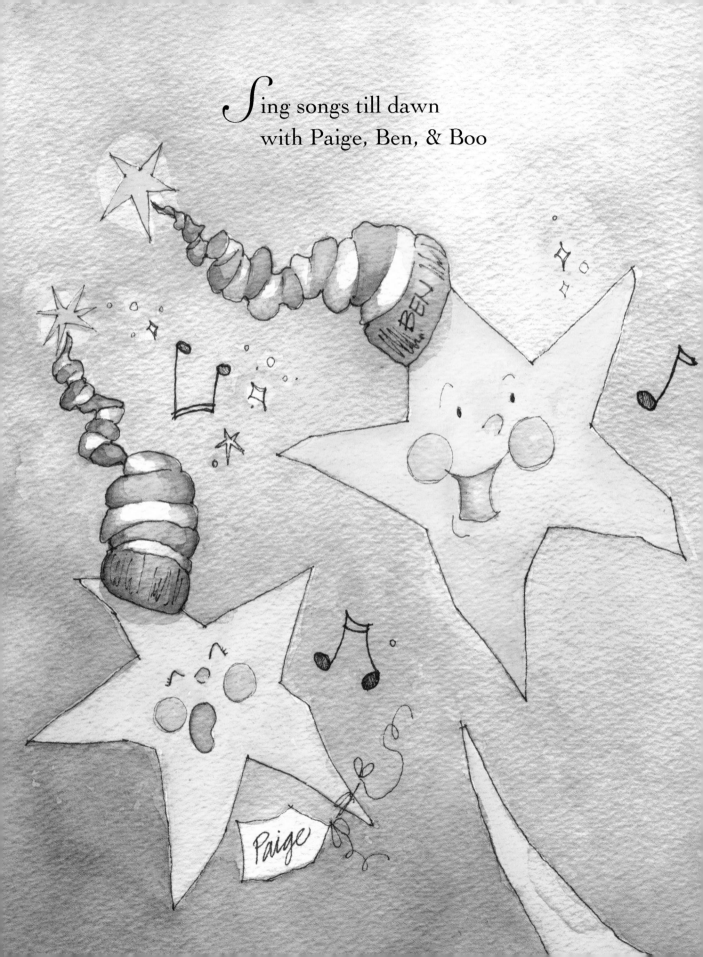

Sing songs till dawn
with Paige, Ben, & Boo

And please,
my dear friend,
take good care
of you.

Now I will sleep cozy all through the night

While you light up stars
like a thousand
white kites.